# A Little Reminder

Words by: Tatsuya Fushimi
Pictures by: Julie Wells

Copyright © 2021 Tatsuya Fushimi.
All rights reserved. No portion of this book may be reproduced, scanned, or distributed in any printed or electronic form without permission.
ISBN: 9781737680901

Cover design and illustrations by Julie Wells.

To Sammy, Jordan, Jacob, Walter Charlie, Nola, Ruby, and Rocky.
You inspire me more than you know.
Love, Tatsu

For Philip, Thea, and Nicholas.
You are so precious to me.
Xoxo, Auntie Julie

I love you.
You are a special gift to this world.
A miracle.
Incredibly unique.

There has never been a person like you before.
There is no one like you now.
There never will be another like you.
Trust me.

Everything about you is beautiful.
Inside and out.

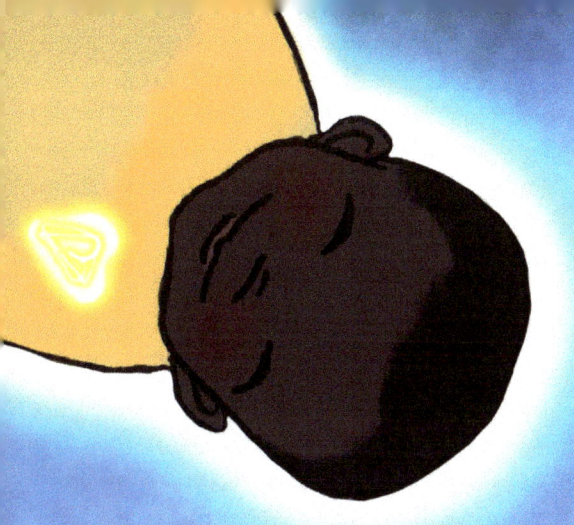

I'm sure of this.
And I'm so proud.

Your eyes.
Your smile.
Your voice.
Your nose.

Your hands.
Your heart.
Your feet.
Your toes.

Your hopes.
Your dreams.
Your spirit.
Your love.

Your likes.
Your dislikes.
Your opinions.
Your hugs.

You are kind.
Smart.
Funny.
Listen closely to me.

You are brave.
Powerful.
Caring.
You are unlimited creativity!

I'm here to support you.
To become the greatest person you want to be.

To share my experiences in this world with you.
And help you explore it safely.

But I'm not perfect, nobody is.
We all make mistakes.
When I do, I'll let you know.
Because honesty is what it takes.

Everything I say and do
Is because I love you.
I'll always do my best for you.
And listen to what you're going through.

I'm so grateful to know you
And to help you make your dreams come true.

So, let's understand each other better.
We've got a lot of exciting things to do!

On your life's journey
Remember these things.

These are some lessons I've learned
That may help your spirit sing.

Most importantly, love yourself.
Be kind to yourself.
Take a deep breath.

Believe in yourself.
Forgive yourself.
Everything always works out in the end.

Take good care of your body.
You only get one.

Sleep well, eat vegetables.
Play and have fun.

Smile big!
Laugh loudly!
Let your energy shine!

Help other people.
And let them help you.
No one succeeds alone.

Here's another thing
That I want you to know.

Never forget this.
Even when you grow old.

You were born with extraordinary gifts.
Gifts still inside of you.

Free them and share them with the world!
It's your responsibility to do!

You were born to help the world.
Wonderful just the way you are.

Listen to the voice in your heart.
And follow it beyond the stars.

Let your dreams and imagination run free!
Farther than your eyes can see!
Go everywhere your heart wants to be!
And believe in every possibility!

I love you.
You are a special gift to this world.
A miracle.
Incredibly unique.

There has never been a person like you before.
There is no one like you now.
There never will be another like you.
Trust me.

# Remember

who you are.

## About the Author

Tatsuya Fushimi is passionate about self-development and is a seeker of his truth. A life coach and entrepreneur, he is inspired to simplify his perspectives gained in adulthood through children's books. His desire is to empower others with more clarity and awareness to help them reach their highest potential. A Southern California native, he enjoys playing golf and engaging in deep conversations about life with everyone he meets.

Instagram: @tatsuyafushimi

## About the Illustrator

Julie Wells is a well-loved children's book illustrator and designer. Her lively and innocent designs remind one of the beauty of childhood. After attending a private Liberal Arts college located in the Shenandoah Valley and earning her Bachelor of Arts in English Literature, Julie began promoting her professional illustration business. She now resides in Virginia, operating Julie Wells Illustration from her home-based studio. Among her illustrated books are Magnificent Meg, Box of Balloons, Henry's Harvest: Apple Cider, and Lightning Bug Lantern.

Instagram: @yourstruliejulie